Martha Bakes a Cake

MARTHA HABLA
Martha hornea un pastel

BILLINGS COUNTY PUBLIC SCHOOL
Box 307
Medora, North Dakota 58645

Adaptation by Karen Barss
Based on a TV series teleplay written by Raye Lankford
Adaptado por Karen Barss. Basado en un guión para televisión escrito por Raye Lankford

Based on the characters created by Susan Meddaugh
Basado en los personajes creados por Susan Meddaugh

Translated by Carlos Calvo   Traducido por Carlos Calvo

HOUGHTON MIFFLIN HARCOURT
Boston • New York • 2012

Ages 5–7 | Grade: 2 | Guided Reading Level: J | Reading Recovery Level: 17 | Spanish Lexile® Level: 390L

ISBN: 978-0-547-71896-5
Design by Rachel Newborn

www.hmhbooks.com | www.marthathetalkingdog.com
Manufactured in Singapore | TWP 10 9 8 7 6 5 4 3 2 1 | 4500343609

Helen is feeling down in the dumps.
Her drawing did not win the art contest.

Helen está deprimida.
No ganó el concurso de arte con su dibujo.

"Your drawing was terrific," says Mom.
"You have to say that. You are my mom," says Helen.

—Tu dibujo era fantástico —le dice su mamá.

—Dices eso porque eres mi mamá —comenta Helen.

Mom drops Helen off at school.

Mamá deja a Helen en la escuela.

Mom wants to cheer up Helen.
At work, Mom has an idea.
"I know," she says. "I will bake her a cake!"

Mamá quiere darle ánimo a Helen.
En el trabajo se le ocurre una idea.
—¡Ya sé! —dice—. ¡Le voy a hornear un pastel!

Licking the bowl will cheer me up!

¡Lamer el tazón me va a dar ánimo a mí!

Just then the phone rings.

Justo entonces suena el teléfono.

Mom gets a big order.
Now she does not have time to bake a cake from scratch.

Mamá recibe un pedido grande.
Y ahora no tiene tiempo para empezar a hornear el pastel.

Martha and Skits run home.
Martha pushes a button.
The TV turns on.

Martha y Skits corren a casa.
Martha presiona un botón.
Se enciende la tele.

They watch Helen's baking DVD.

Miran el DVD de cocina de Helen.

"First, collect your ingredients," says the TV cook.

—Primero, consigan los ingredientes —dice la cocinera de la tele.

"To start, you need eggs, milk, and butter."

—Para empezar, necesitan huevos, leche y mantequilla.

Martha and Skits go into the kitchen.
Skits grabs a milk carton.
His teeth make holes and it leaks.

Martha y Skits van a la cocina.
Skits agarra un cartón de leche.
Sus dientes hacen agujeros y la leche gotea.

He takes it to the living room.
Skits drops it on the floor.

Lo lleva a la sala.
Skits lo deja caer al suelo.

He goes back to the kitchen.
Skits grabs an egg carton.
He drops it next to the milk.

Vuelve a la cocina.
Skits agarra un cartón de huevos.
Lo deja caer al lado de la leche.

All the eggs crack!

¡Todos los huevos se rompen!

Martha rings the neighbor's doorbell.

Martha toca el timbre de su vecina.

I know she will help us.
Sé que nos va a ayudar.

Mrs. Parkington opens the door.
"May we borrow two eggs,
please?" asks Martha.

La Sra. Parkington abre la puerta.
—¿Nos puede dar dos huevos, por
favor? —le pregunta Martha.

Martha and Skits walk home holding the eggs.

Martha y Skits regresan a casa llevando los huevos.

A squirrel runs by as they near
the door.
Both dogs drop their eggs to bark.

Cuando se acercan a la puerta, una ardilla pasa corriendo.
Los dos perros dejan caer los huevos para ladrarle.

Oh, bummer.
¡Qué lata!

Martha knows what to do.
"More eggs? What next? Flour? Milk?" asks Mrs. Parkington.
"Now that you mention it," says Martha.

Martha sabe lo que tiene que hacer.
—¿Más huevos? ¿Qué más? ¿Harina? ¿Leche? —pregunta la Sra. Parkington.
—Ahora que lo menciona... —dice Martha.

Thanks, again.
Gracias de nuevo.

Mrs. Parkington puts everything in a wagon.
Then she pulls the wagon to Martha's house so the
ingredients do not spill.

La Sra. Parkington pone los ingredientes en un carrito.
Luego lleva el carrito hasta la casa de Martha para que no se
caigan los ingredientes.

Then Martha and Skits get to work.
"Pour the ingredients into a bowl," says the TV cook.
"Stir well."

Después, Martha y Skits se ponen a trabajar.
—Viertan los ingredientes en un tazón —dice la cocinera de la tele—. Revuelvan bien.

Martha wants to pour the flour into her dog dish.
She spills it all over.

Martha quiere verter los ingredientes en el plato donde come.
Y lo derrama todo.

"Let's just mix everything here on the rug," says Martha.

—Mezclémoslo todo en la alfombra —dice Martha.

So Martha and Skits pour out all the ingredients.
They blend them together with their paws.

Entonces Martha y Skits vierten todos los ingredientes.
Y los mezclan con las patas.

Then they push the batter into Martha's bowl.

Luego arrastran la mezcla hasta el plato donde come Martha.

"Looking good!" says Martha.

—¡Se ve bien! —dice Martha.

Martha and Skits get the batter into the pan.

Martha y Skits ponen la mezcla en el molde.

The dogs are covered with flour.
They shake it off.
Then they push the cake pan into the kitchen. But how will Martha and Skits bake the cake?

Los perros quedan cubiertos de harina.
Se la sacuden.
Después arrastran el molde hasta la cocina.
¿Pero cómo lo van a hacer Martha y Skits para hornear el pastel?

We can't turn on the oven!
¡No podemos encender el horno!

Luckily, Howie the mailman comes to the door.
"Howie," says Martha, "can you help us?"

Por suerte llega Howie, el cartero.
—Howie —le pide Martha—, ¿nos puedes ayudar?

Martha asks Howie to turn on the oven and put in the cake.
After Howie leaves, Martha says, "In thirty minutes, we take out the cake."

Martha le pide a Howie que encienda el horno y ponga el pastel dentro.
Cuando Howie se va, Martha dice: —Lo sacaremos en treinta minutos.

Then Martha calls Wagstaff City Pizza.
"Can you deliver a pizza in thirty minutes?"
she asks.

Entonces Martha llama a Wagstaff
City Pizza.
—¿Me puede traer una pizza en
treinta minutos? —pregunta.

When the pizza delivery boy
comes, Martha asks him to take
out the cake.

Cuando llega el repartidor de pizzas,
Martha le pide que saque el pastel.

Just then, Helen and Mom come home.

En ese momento, Helen y su mamá llegan a casa.

Surprise!
¡Sorpresa!

"We baked you a cake to cheer you up!" cries Martha.

—¡Hemos horneado un pastel para darte ánimo! —grita Martha.

Dad comes in. "Who wants cake?" he asks.

Llega papá.
—¿Quién quiere pastel? —pregunta.

But we made a cake!
¡Pero nosotros hicimos un pastel!

"What if I eat Dad's cake," asks
Helen, "and keep yours forever?"

—¿Qué tal si comemos el pastel que trajo
papá —le pregunta Helen— y guardamos
el tuyo para siempre?

"That would be a waste of cake," says Martha.
Skits barks.
"Great idea, Skits," says Martha.

—Sería un desperdicio de pastel —dice Martha.
Skits ladra.
—Buena idea, Skits —dice Martha.